Arthur and the Comet Crisis

A Marc Brown ARTHUR Chapter Book

Arthur and the Comet Crisis

Text by Stephen Krensky

Based on a teleplay by Peter Hirsch

Little, Brown and Company

Boston   New York   London

Text has been reviewed and assigned a reading level by Laurel S. Ernst, M.A., Teachers College, Columbia University, New York, New York; reading specialist, Chappaqua, New York.

ISBN 0-316-12462-1 (hc) / 0-316-12199-1 (pb)

LCCN 2002102897

10 9 8 7 6 5 4 3 2 1

WOR (hc)
COM-MO (pb)

Printed in the United States of America

For my sister Colleen

Chapter 1

• • • • • • • • • •

As Arthur arrived at school one morning, Fern came up beside him.

"Hi, Arthur," she said.

"Mmmmmmm," Arthur mumbled.

"I see you overslept," Fern went on.

Arthur blinked at her. "Huh? What makes you say that?"

"You're wearing two different-colored socks and your sweater's on inside-out. Why?" She pointed a finger at him. "Because you slept late!"

Arthur looked stunned. "You're right! That's amazing."

Fern tapped the book she was holding.

"I'm reading *Mrs. Marbles's Handbook for Young Detectives*. Deduction is all in the details."

Just then Buster came running up.

"Arthur! Hey, Arthur!"

Fern consulted her book. "Aha! Panting . . . a look of urgency. . . . He's trying to tell us something."

Buster ignored her. "It's happened, Arthur, it's finally happened!"

"What?" asked Arthur.

"I saw a —" He stopped himself and looked around suspiciously. "Wait! Not here. They might be listening."

"Who?" said Arthur.

"The aliens."

Arthur thought for a moment. "Are they powerful?" he asked.

"Of course," said Buster.

"Technologically advanced?"

"Definitely."

Arthur tried not to smile. "So they'll

hear us no matter where you tell me, right?"

Buster stopped to think. "I guess. . . . Well, I'd just gone to bed, when all of a sudden I heard a strange noise."

Buster was lying in bed holding his stuffed Bionic Bunny. He could hear a pulsing sound outside. He went to the window and raised the blinds. Suddenly, multicolored lights spilled into the room.

"And there it was — as plain as day. It was round and silvery with blinking lights. My first real UFO!"

"Wait a minute," said Arthur. "I thought you saw a UFO last week."

"No, no," Buster said, "that was just the little light on the smoke alarm. This was the real thing. They flew right over my house."

"They?" said Fern. "Just how many UFOs were there?"

"Um . . . three. No, make that six. I don't

know. There were a lot of them. Anyway, I went downstairs. . . ."

The grass looked red and blue and green in the light of the saucers. Buster walked outside, still in his pajamas and holding his Bionic Bunny. A UFO hovered just above the apartment rooftop, with countless other UFOs behind it.

"Then they made this weird vibrating noise. It wasn't like anything I'd ever heard before."

The Brain, who had come up while Buster was speaking, started laughing.

"What?" said Buster sharply.

"Come on, Buster," said the Brain. "It was probably just a plane."

"Or maybe a helicopter," said Fern.

"Oh, yeah?" Buster folded his arms. "Could a plane or a helicopter beam you up and take you two hundred million light years away?"

"Is that what happened next?" asked Fern.

"Well, no," Buster admitted, "but it could have. You have to believe me. I really did see something last night."

"I hate to tell you this, Buster," said the Brain, "but UFOs don't exist."

"How do you know? They could."

"There's no concrete evidence for them. Just a lot of crazy theories."

"Th-they're not crazy theories!" Buster sputtered. "They're good theories made up by normal people like me."

He started for the classroom. "You'll see! I'll get proof. Then we'll see who has the shoe on the other hand."

He went in, slamming the classroom door behind him.

Chapter 2

Late that afternoon, Arthur was in his tree house pulling a rope through the doorway.

"Ngggh! Nggggggh!"

"Just a little more," said Buster.

"It would be easier," said Arthur, "if this thing wasn't so heavy."

The rope Arthur was pulling on was tied around a big cardboard box. Buster was lifting it from underneath, but the box was very heavy.

"It'll be worth it," groaned Buster. "You'll see."

With a final heave from both Buster and

Arthur, the box scraped through the doorway into the tree house and tumbled off to one side.

Arthur sighed with relief. "Phew! Leave it to Muffy to have the world's largest telescope. I still don't see why we had to lug this all the way up here. Couldn't we have used it on the ground?"

"Higher is better," said Buster. "It means we're closer to the action." He pulled off some tape and opened the box. "Wow! This is brand new. Never been used."

Arthur took a look. "It's in pieces," he said. "Lots of pieces."

"Not for long," said Buster. "Here are the instructions."

He pulled out a pamphlet and opened it. "Uh-oh. This looks complicated."

"Just start at the beginning," said Arthur. "I'm sure we can figure it out."

"Okay. Place the ETX-90/EC refractor on the azimuth mount."

"I said the beginning, Buster."

"That is the beginning. See?" He showed Arthur the top of the page.

Arthur sighed. "I guess this is what they mean by 'Some assembly required.' "

They started working. Most of the pieces went on easily, but some took a little longer. Neither of them noticed, though, when one knob rolled onto the floor and dropped through the doorway and onto the ground.

Hours later, Arthur made the last twist with the screwdriver. He and Buster stood back to admire their work.

"It sure is a beauty," said Buster.

The huge telescope was more than just a big tube of glass and metal. It had a little computer, a printer, and a digital camera sitting beneath the eyepiece.

Arthur took the first look.

"What do you see?" asked Buster.

"Well, the moon is rising. I can see craters. . . . Hey, there's this old guy waving at me."

"Really? Oh . . . very funny. Let me look."

Buster took so long that Arthur sat back and closed his eyes.

"Whoa!"

Arthur got up, excited. "What? What?"

"Mr. Haney has purple pajamas."

"Buster, you're supposed to be looking at the sky!"

"Oh, yeah."

Arthur yawned. "I think I've seen enough for now. I'm going inside. Are you coming?"

"I think I'll stay a little longer."

"Okay. Bye." Arthur climbed down from the tree house while Buster continued to look through the telescope.

"Wow! Look at — oh, it's a plane. Wait a minute! What's that?"

He pressed a button on the telescope, and the camera took its first picture.

Chapter 3

* * * * * * * * * * *

The Brain was eating lunch in the school cafeteria when Buster walked up and stood before him.

"You need to stop eating for a moment," he said.

"I do?" said the Brain. "Why?"

"So you can feast your eyes on *this*."

He thrust a photograph under the Brain's nose.

The Brain examined the picture. "It's very nice," he said. "Good composition."

Buster waved the photo. "Never mind the composition! You wanted proof of a UFO. Now you've got it."

"That's not proof," said the Brain. "That's a shooting star. Or, in more scientific terms, a small object, such as a meteoroid, entering the Earth's atmosphere and burning up."

"Hmph!" Buster snatched the photo back and stomped away. "I'm not done yet. We'll see who's an uncle's monkey, Mr. Smarty-Pants."

The next day at the library, the Brain was cleaning the book-return counter when the door opened.

"Prepare yourself!" cried Buster.

"*Ssssh!*" said the Brain. "This is a library, remember?"

"Have it your way," Buster whispered. "Prepare yourself."

The Brain folded his arms. "For what?"

Buster brought out several photographs and held up the one on top. "For this!" he declared.

The Brain took a look. He yawned. "That's not a UFO, Buster."

"How can you say that? It's much too big to be a star."

"True," said the Brain. "And too big to be a spacecraft, as well. Actually, it's Jupiter."

"Jupiter?"

"The planet. You know, the biggest one in our solar system."

"Yeah, yeah, I've heard of it." He frowned. "Okay, then, what about this?"

He took out another picture.

"Ah, well," said the Brain, "that's definitely not a star or a planet."

"What did I tell you?" said Buster.

"It's the Crosswire Blimp. I read in the newspaper that Muffy's father was starting a new ad campaign for his dealership."

"A blimp?" Buster's face fell. "I was so sure . . ."

"Buster, you have to remember, the night sky is filled with all kinds of things."

"What about legs?"

"Legs?"

"Yes, legs. Do you see a lot of legs in the night sky?"

"No," the Brain admitted, "I guess not."

"Then how about this, Mr. Answer Man?" He handed his last picture to the Brain.

"Well, well . . ."

"Not a planet, is it?" said Buster.

"Nope."

"Not a blimp, either," Buster went on.

"Nope," the Brain said again.

Buster smiled. "Then how do you explain the legs?"

"It's a fly."

"A fly?" Buster laughed. "How would a fly get into space?"

"It wouldn't," said the Brain. "It must

have been sitting on the lens when you took the picture."

The Brain stood up and got a book from one of the shelves.

"Here," he said. "This is a book on astronomy. Instead of asking me questions every five minutes, why don't you just see if there's a picture of it in here first? If you're still confused, then we can talk."

Buster took the book and slunk away. At that moment, he didn't feel like talking to anyone.

Chapter 4

• • • • • • • • • • • •

That evening Buster sat alone in the tree house, eating an apple from the basket of food his mother had just brought him.

"I'll show the Brain," he muttered to himself. "He's not the only one around here who knows something about star power. I know the moon when I see it, and I know it's not made of green cheese." He paused. "At least I don't think it is, because if it was, wouldn't a lot of mice live there?"

He looked through the telescope.

"Blinking light. . . . That's a plane. . . . More blinking lights. . . . Hey! What's that?"

He snapped the camera button, and a moment later the picture came out of the printer. It showed a bright, fuzzy ball with a long, white tail.

Buster picked up the astronomy book and flipped through it. He came to a page with a picture much like the one in his hand.

"Oh, it's just a comet. Nothing special about that. Unless, of course, it's a very clever UFO pretending to be a comet on the outside while on the inside it's an alien invasion spaceship."

He started to read aloud.

"Comets are big pieces of dirty ice . . . blah, blah, blah . . . only rarely found by amateur astronomers."

Buster paused. He knew it wouldn't be easy to put a spaceship inside a giant snowball, but who could be sure what these aliens were capable of?

He continued reading.

"To calculate the orbit of the comet, observe its movement over a period of days."

Buster looked up. That might be good to do. If it didn't act like a regular comet, then he would know that aliens were involved.

For the next three nights, Buster took a new picture of the comet at exactly eight o'clock. He didn't say anything to his friends about this because he didn't want them laughing at him again. "All I need is proof of something," he told himself, "and they won't be laughing anymore."

After taking the three pictures, Buster sat down at the telescope and read from the instruction manual. Once he fed in all the data he had collected on the comet, the computer would do some computing, and the screen would show him the comet's projected path.

"Let's see. . . . That's everything. . . . Now press F12."

He pressed the button, and a map of the solar system filled the computer screen. A flashing dot was moving across it, getting closer and closer to the Earth.

"That shows the comet's path so far, and one more step will show where it's going."

He pressed another button and the flashing lights changed from green to red. As Buster watched in disbelief, the red lights continued on a straight line until they hit the Earth.

"Warning!" said the computer. "The object at right ascension three-point-six hours plus twenty degrees will collide with Earth in five weeks. Have a nice day."

Buster blinked. "Huh?" he said.

Chapter 5

At dinner that night, Buster didn't eat very much. He wasn't just sitting at the table doing nothing, though. He had shaped his mashed potatoes into a ball and was dropping peas on it, one at a time.

"Buster?"

He looked up. "Yes, Mom?"

"Why are you doing that?"

Buster frowned. "Doing what?"

His mother sighed. "You keep dropping peas on your mashed potatoes. And every time the pea hits, you make this exploding sound."

"I do?"

She nodded. *"BRRRRCCCHHHHHH!* Or something like that. One time for every pea."

Buster looked down and counted. There were twelve peas stuck in his mashed potatoes.

"Mom, do you know what would happen if a comet hit the Earth?"

Mrs. Baxter thought for a moment.

"It would depend on its size — and where it hit. There would be a giant explosion when the comet hit either the ground or the water. In the ocean, there would be a follow-up tidal wave for sure. A large explosion in the ground could raise a dust cloud bigger than the biggest skyscraper. This dust could be blown by the wind, blocking the sunlight like a blanket."

"Would it last a long time?"

"It might. Some of the dust thrown up by volcanoes has taken years to settle down again. If the dust stayed up long enough, it could lead to another ice age. Some people believe that a comet colliding with the Earth over sixty million years ago is what caused the dinosaurs to die out. Why do you ask?"

"Oh, just curious."

Buster got up calmly and walked into the kitchen. He replayed the telescope computer's words in his mind. *The object at right ascension three-point-six hours plus twenty degrees will collide with Earth in five weeks.*

Then he dumped his silverware in the trash and put his empty plate in the refrigerator. He had thought about going back to the telescope for another look, but somehow he didn't seem to have enough energy to make the trip.

Buster knew he must have spent the evening doing something, but he couldn't remember afterward what it was. All he remembered was that it took him a really long time to put on his pajamas. In the end, he only got it right after he realized he had been repeatedly trying to put the bottoms over his head.

He did remember looking out the window and noticing how peaceful everything was. The trees, the park, even the sidewalks seemed so solid and comfortable.

And the whole time, he kept on murmuring to himself, "The comet is coming, the comet is coming."

When his mother came in to kiss him good-night, he barely noticed. She asked if he was feeling sick, but he just said, "No." There was no point in worrying her, not yet, anyway.

Then he lay on his side and stared at his wall, which was fading in and out as he got more and more tired. "The comet is coming, the comet is coming," he said softly for the hundredth time.

And then he fell asleep.

Chapter 6

● ● ● ● ● ● ● ● ● ● ●

In the Oval Office, the president was sitting behind his presidential desk. How he wished he could put the desk in a corner — he liked corners — but there weren't any in the Oval Office, so he had to make do. The desk was covered with a lot of presidential stuff, but President Baxter wasn't paying much attention to it.

A general stood before him. "Mr. President, the latest figures predict that the comet will hit the Earth in only one hour."

The president swiveled in his chair to look out the window. "All of our defenses, have they been —"

"We tried, Mr. President, believe me. Our greatest scientists, led by the Brain, made this their top priority."

"Ah, yes, the Brain thinks he knows so much."

"There's a reason for that, sir," said the general.

"Oh, really?" said President Baxter. "What is it?"

"It's because he really does know so much."

President Baxter walked to the window. "And did it help, all this knowledge he supposedly has?"

"No, sir, I'm afraid not. Under his direction, we sent up everything we had. None of it worked. The comet is just too big, too powerful."

"Then we have only one chance."

The general came to attention. "Yes, sir. Bionic Bunny is standing by, waiting for your order."

"Send him. Send him now!"

Far out in space, Bionic Bunny raced toward the comet. He could still hear the words of the president ringing in his ears, how it was up to him to save the world once again.

At the great speed he was traveling, he came up to the comet quickly. It was just beyond the last traces of Earth's atmosphere. The view even made him pause. The comet was huge, massive — Bionic Bunny felt like a bug facing the biggest windshield in the universe. Still, he did not hesitate. The whole world was depending on him, and he was not about to let everyone down.

"It's now or never," he said.

Clenching his fists, he flew up to the comet and tried to break it into smaller pieces.

But the comet was so cold, so frozen, that it withstood his mighty blows.

Bionic Bunny then tried to push against the comet, trying to change its direction. The comet stayed on course.

"Can't . . . give . . . up . . . yet!" he groaned.

But the comet paid no attention.

"Too much forward momentum. But I'm not done with this overgrown snowball yet."

He flew around to the back of the comet, grabbed the comet's tail — and pulled.

"Yes! It's slowing down."

Just then the international space station passed by, and one of its solar panels got snagged on Bionic Bunny's cape. It yanked him away and allowed the comet to resume its plunge toward Earth.

"Noooooooo!" he cried.

But out in space, no one could hear him.

Chapter 7

At school the next morning, some of the students arrived on their bikes. As always, they parked them in the racks, took off their helmets, and went inside.

When Buster got to school, he was wearing his bike helmet, too. But he didn't head for the racks, because he didn't need to. He wasn't riding his bike.

A few kids on the playground stared at him as he passed by.

"What's up, Buster?"

"Not feeling so safe today?"

"Earth to Buster, come in, Buster."

None of these comments drew any

replies. In fact, it wasn't clear that Buster even heard them. He was too tired from remembering each and every moment of his dream. He had awakened after Bionic Bunny had been pulled away from the comet, so he had not seen what had happened next. But he could imagine. And if he had slept again afterward, he hadn't slept well.

Inside Mr. Ratburn's classroom, Buster stumbled to his seat and sat down.

"*Pssst!* Buster!"

Buster looked up. Arthur seemed to be speaking to him. But why was he whispering?

"Your bike helmet . . ."

Buster frowned. "What about it?"

"Um . . . it's still on."

"Oh."

Buster took off his helmet.

"Are you all right?" Arthur asked. "You look kind of funny."

Buster grabbed Arthur's sleeve.

"Don't panic, Arthur, but a comet is coming."

"Coming? Coming where?"

"Here," said Buster. "Planet Earth. There's going to be a big explosion. Another ice age. Lots of stuff will be wiped out. Pass it on."

Arthur tried to keep his mouth from dropping open too far. "Oh-kay," he said.

At recess, Arthur walked up to Fern. "Did you hear the news about the comet?"

"Yup." She looked in her notebook. "I'm keeping track of all the facts — strange headgear in the classroom, a belief that the sky is falling. . . . I hate to say this, Arthur, but Mrs. Marbles would conclude that Buster has finally lost his cookies."

"He's definitely upset, that's for sure." Arthur looked around. "Uh-oh. I don't think he's done yet."

Buster had climbed to the top of the monkey bars and was calling for everyone's attention.

"LISTEN UP, PEOPLE! A COMET IS COMING! IT WILL DESTROY A LOT. MAYBE EVEN US. WE NEED A PLAN — AND FAST!"

For a moment, the students looked at Buster without moving. Then the moment passed, and they all went back to whatever they were doing before.

"DIDN'T YOU HEAR WHAT I SAID?"

The kids went on playing.

"HEY! THIS IS SERIOUS!"

"Yeah, yeah, a comet's coming," said one kid. "I can't wait to tell the tooth fairy."

Everyone laughed. Buster looked shocked, wounded. Nobody was listening to him. It wouldn't be long before they would have to listen because the comet would be darkening the sky.

But by then it would be too late.

Chapter 8

. . . .

"Well, I tried."

Buster said this as he sat at the counter of the ice-cream shop drinking a double-thick chocolate shake.

"Tough day?" asked the Brain's mother, who was working behind the counter.

Buster sighed. "I'll say. You'd think people would pay attention when you were telling them about a comet hitting the Earth. You'd think they would care."

"I think Binky was listening," said the Brain, who was sweeping the floor behind him. He often helped his mother out by working in her shop after school.

Buster snorted. "Sort of. He just said he wasn't going to work on any long-term homework projects if he didn't have to. I'm not sure that counts."

"Well," said the Brain, "things might have gone better if you had taken off your bike helmet. When someone talks about the end of the world while wearing a bike helmet, people don't always pay attention."

"Hey, I wasn't wearing it for protection," Buster explained. "I was trying to make a point."

"And did you?"

"Well, no. . . . But I would have if everyone hadn't been shouting 'Chicken Little' at me."

The Brain nodded. "I admit that didn't help. Clearly, you need to adopt a different approach."

"Maybe you're right," said Buster.

"You're still wearing it, you know," said the Brain.

"Wearing what?"

"Your bike helmet."

"Oh." Buster undid the strap and took the helmet off.

"That's a good start," said the Brain.

Buster didn't look so sure. "I don't know. Maybe I'm not the right person for the job. Maybe this news should be coming from someone else."

"Like who?"

"Someone the kids respect."

"Sounds good."

Buster took a deep breath. "Someone they know would be telling the truth."

"That sounds good, too."

Buster suddenly smiled. "Someone like . . . you!"

"Me?" The Brain looked horrified. "Why me?"

"You'd be perfect. Everyone knows you're smart and serious. They'll believe you for sure, because you sound so sciencey."

The Brain snorted. "That's because I back up what I say with facts, unlike some people. And 'sciencey' isn't a word, anyway."

"Exactly." Buster grinned. "See, you picked right up on that."

"Yes, well, you may have figured out why everyone will believe me. But you still have a problem."

"What's that?"

The Brain folded his arms. "How are you going to get me to believe you? Why should I go around telling people a comet is coming?"

Buster began fishing in his backpack. "Because I have proof! Look!" He took the picture of the comet and handed it to the Brain. The Brain took a good look.

"Well, it does appear to be a comet. But that's not enough. There are dates to confirm and trajectories to check. I'll have to sift through all your data."

"No problem," said Buster. "It's in the tree house." He paid for his milkshake, grabbed his helmet, and dragged the Brain toward the door. "Come on," he said, "we've only got thirty-five-and-a-half days left."

Chapter 9

● ● ● ● ● ● ● ● ● ● ● ●

That evening, Arthur, Muffy, Francine, Fern, and Binky were all standing at the base of the clubhouse tree. They were looking at Buster, who was pacing the ground before them.

"Do you realize I had to cancel a hairstyling to be here?" said Muffy.

"Don't worry," said Buster. "Your hair will still be around tomorrow."

"Well," said Francine, "Fern and I were supposed to go shopping."

"There's a sale on magnifying glasses and fingerprint pads," said Fern. "I was going to stock up."

"We all had plans, Buster," said Arthur.

"Yeah," said Binky. "I was supposed to be cleaning my room." He paused. "Oh, I guess this isn't so bad. Keep talking, Buster."

"As I was saying, you're here because I asked you to come."

"And also because the Brain asked," Francine reminded him. "But neither of you would say why. Hey, this doesn't have anything to do with that crazy comet talk, does it?"

"At least you took off that helmet," said Muffy. "Talk about a fashion mistake!"

Arthur shivered. "Buster, are you sure this couldn't have waited until tomorrow? It's cold out here."

Buster glanced up at the tree house. "Just be patient. This is important. You'll see."

"Can't you give us a clue?" asked Fern. "I'm very good with clues."

"Maybe he won't," said the Brain,

climbing down the ladder. "But I will. You were right, Francine. This does have to do with the comet."

Francine frowned. "I knew it. I knew we were wasting our time."

The Brain sighed. "I only wish that were true."

Everyone suddenly got quiet.

"What do you mean?" Arthur asked.

"If . . . we're . . . not . . . wasting . . . our . . . time," began Muffy, "that . . . means . . ."

"Exactly," said the Brain. "I have checked all of Buster's findings and examined the three photographs he took. And according to my calculations . . . he's right! There really is a comet heading toward Earth."

"AAAAAAAHHHHHHH!"

It was hard to say who screamed first or who was screaming the loudest because everyone was screaming. They pointed at the sky, the ground, and each other.

Only Buster stood calmly by. "There!" he said. "Now do you believe me?"

"Comet! Comet! Comet!" yelled Fern, who had started to pace. Suddenly she stepped on something. "Ow!"

She bent down and picked up the metal knob that had accidentally fallen through the tree-house doorway days earlier.

"Hmmmm. Could this be a real clue?" She looked up at the tree house opening above her. "Mrs. Marbles would say, 'The obvious possibility is almost always the first one checked.'"

And so as everyone else argued about what to do, Fern quietly climbed the tree-house ladder. There was a mystery here somewhere, and she was determined to solve it.

Chapter 10

In the Sugar Bowl the next day, D.W. and Arthur sat in a booth facing Fern.

"And then?" asked D.W., taking a bite out of her muffin.

"And then," said Fern, "using my little gray brain cells" — she tapped her head — "I determined that the curious metal knob was actually an important part of the telescope, and without it, Buster and the Brain were getting all the wrong readings. So I quickly climbed up the tree and —"

"And," said Arthur, "we fixed the telescope and discovered the comet wasn't going to hit Earth after all. The end."

"I like the story better when Fern tells it," said D.W. "Tell it again. And don't rush the part where Arthur runs around like a chicken."

"No!" cried Arthur. "No more!"

At that moment Buster and the Brain entered.

"Here it is!" cried Buster, holding up a newspaper. "What a headline! CAT SAVER DISCOVERS COMET."

"That's fine for you, Buster," said the Brain, holding a newspaper of his own, "but they spelled my name wrong. They called me 'the Bran.' It makes me sound like breakfast cereal."

"It turns out," said Buster, "that I'm not the only amateur to discover something in space. A girl named Heather McCurdy discovered a planetoid with her friends."

"It's still pretty amazing that you discovered a comet, Buster," said Arthur.

"Hardly any ordinary people have ever done that before."

"I guess so. I just wish it was going to come back sooner. Once it passes by, we won't see it again for another three years."

The Brain put down his newspaper. "Well, who knows? Maybe they will have discovered alien life-forms by then."

Buster gaped at him. "You mean . . . you're now a believer?"

"Not exactly," said the Brain. "But . . ."

"But what?" Buster demanded.

"Well," said the Brain, "I've made an important discovery."

"What's that?" asked Arthur.

The Brain smiled. "If there's intelligent life up here," he said, pointing to Buster's head, "then clearly it could be anywhere."